I0771409

Detective Novel

Craig Rodgers

Thank you to Tex Gresham for another excellent cover design.

Death of Print is a sort of imprint of Malarkey Books dedicated to bringing out books that were nearly lost. Generally that means their original publisher shut down, but in the case of Detective Novel the manuscript was nearly lost in a fire. This book only exists because, somehow, the notebook pages did not burn up. Both publisher and author are grateful to you for reading it and the fire gods for sparing it.

malarkeybooks.com

Also by Craig Rodgers:

The Ghost of Mile 43
Moonbeams
Twenty Ponds
One More Number
Francis Top's Grand Design
Drift
The Mountain Is Burning Down
Clutch 1900
Oriel
Francis Top's Lost Cipher

Before

The bridge leans at a cant awkward and unnatural. Bolts not yet rusted and gone cling to their antique moorings. Wooden planks in spots have rotted and fallen away leaving gaps where only iron skeleton remains. Someday the last points gripped will give in and the works in its entirety will go tumbling into the river but that day is not today.

The man who steps onto the bridge moves along with a surety that dares the broken nature of each yard trespassed. There is more or less a midpoint in this twisted relic and at that inferred axis the man stops and he turns and somewhere below waters come onward as they forever have.

He bows to pull at the string of one oxford and he removes that shoe and then he repeats this with the other. The pair he sets on a board warped and gray at his side. Upright again. He breathes in, he breathes out. He blinks at some thought meant for him alone. Then he is removing a cufflink and rolling up a sleeve and he is removing the next, rolling up the next. The links are together loosed with the barest of tosses to disappear beneath the current in a thump too slight to hear.

There is a moment. Not a hesitation but a moment of waiting. Then he is taking a step and he is falling and there is another thump in the water and he is gone.

Among the trees on the other side of the river there stands a bearded stranger, a transient in a coat long and worn, new stitching over old in thread of brown or green on fabric gone black to gray. He has only just arrived or maybe he watched, maybe he has been here all along. The transient with his beard and old coat steps from the greenery and he crosses open grass and with deft stride he moves along the bridge to where the shined oxfords wait. He lowers his frame to that warped lumber and one shoe after another he measures against worn sneaker with sole walked to nub. It's near enough. He nods to himself and he stands and he goes and with his passing a calm soon returns to this forgotten halcyon setting.

————

Now

————

1. A Missing Man

It's there in the paper, and then it isn't. The disappearance of one Calvin Lond. Scant details, quotes from neighbors, friends. A photo of him with an old man, his father, alongside the vital youth of the figure now lost. The story gives no updates because there are no updates to be had.

Linus stares at a screen. He's read all about it on the paper's website. The Oriel Courant. Accounts of events as seen or believed. He read about it then and he reads about it still, weeks gone by, the stark oddness of it. This man gone. Swallowed by creation.

Somewhere deeper in the building a phone rings unending. There are voices somewhere. The idea of voices. In the depths. The warehouse or the press where machinery once chugged. The walls carry these phantoms along.

The missing man. Lond. Linus stirs. He has what he thinks are the beginnings of an idea. Somewhere in the building another phone begins ringing, each toll echoing along empty hallways. It goes on and on. Minutes. He is undeterred. He examines each story again and again. This is something. The missing man, already forgotten. This is something.

———

The house has spilled onto the lawn. Debris of expended years, end tables and bureaus and divans. These innards of personal minutiae have been arranged in a frenzied wash along the grass out front of the bland, overlarge suburban home planted among miles of the same stretching off in every direction.

An old man sits on a bench. Aged iron bars twisted gothic ornate. Stained wood slats warped and weathered. Linus approaches. He puts a hand out.

"Mr. Lond?"

The old man takes the hand and squeezes. Skin like paper left out in the weather. Linus says what's all this and the old man says who're you and Linus tells a lie, he says I am a journalist.

"You're selling his things?"

"He won't need them."

"Why is that?"

"Hmm."

"You're sure he's not coming back?"

The old man shrugs and turns away. He says look around. He says everything is for sale.

Others come and go. Gawkers drawn to pick through the leavings of the vanished. They shake hands with the old man, or they fondle the dusty surface of a thing left inert without the being of its former keeper. Neighbors slip out of their houses to meander through the arrangement like the lost in some lackluster maze.

Linus walks among the scattered mass. He falls into a chair of antique wood and dark felt alongside a trunk and desk of similar vintage. Their browsing circles all around. He crosses one leg over the other. He takes out a notepad, a pen. A woman in a business suit of smart cut picks up a stone block from a table and she turns it in her hands and sets it back. A man in a tracksuit removes thick glasses and leans down to take in the details of an armoire. Linus taps pen on pad. He looks down at the page as if something will have changed there but it has not.

The engine is heard from far off. A rumble falling and rising. Linus turns, the old man turns, others. A car comes along riding the din. An old coupe painted a shining turquoise, waxed and loved since its 1940 birth. Whitewalls, fender skirts. It stops and turns around and slides in at the curb. The man who steps out onto the street is immaculate. The checkered slacks of an old time dandy. Hair slicked hard away. He wears the pale skin and baby face of a silent film star. And he smiles, and he smiles. He steps onto grass and he moves among the baubles gathered.

The pale man enters the maze. He does as the others do, touching old photos of strangers, ogling antiques displayed. His eyes shift along objects and faces, scanning like an animal. Those eyes meet Linus' and they move on and return. He straightens.

"What're you?"

The old man turns in his seat.

"Oh, that's a reporter."

A moment passes. The pale man is only standing, only smiling. The gawkers begin to turn, anticipating. Then the moment has ended and he moves on.

He comes down rows and around and there he finds the block of stone. He leans down, he runs a hand across its face. A black piece of rock carved and polished, streaks of color running like the memory of an older earth. The pale man hefts the black hunk of rock.

"Is this worth anything?"

The old man shifts again and turns around to see.

"Make me an offer."

"It doesn't have a price."

"It costs what you buy it for. There isn't gonna be a going rate. It was a kind of trophy. An award."

"It meant something to him."

The old man nods.

"He loved that thing."

The pale man lifts the object again. He feels the weight of the thing and he nods.

"I thank you kindly."

He crosses the lawn in confident step. The old man says hey. He stands up and says hey again. The pale man bends down into the coupe and the engine becomes a roar. The old man is still shouting but no one hears. The maze is unchanged, the gawkers still gawk among its pillars. Linus stands at the periphery of these doings. He squints. He scribbles in his notebook. License plate digits. The coupe howls as it pulls away.

Everything is public. He scrolls his phone and he pays a fee and it's all there. Coupe, registration, owner. Jeremy Red. The address is a business. Mini Mall.

Suburbs and the city to which they are bound fall away behind Linus as miles of open highway carry him in his sagging heap past rolled hay and a lot for RVs and churches for all manner of god. Truck stops and vast stretches of nothing and a cast-off train car on a block foundation. He crosses over a border marked by a sign of green aluminum stamped with a word. Oriel. The day has begun its fall into evening. Off the highway he passes another sign, wood now, carved and painted again with the town name. Alongside this word there is etched in some detail a ship held forever in a bottle laid on its side. Linus drives on.

Blocks go by with their small town layers, eras displayed in shift from one style to another. Too small to be districts. Neighborhoods. A mechanical voice guides the way. Turn here, go there, four hundred feet. It leads him downtown. A strip center, lined-up storefronts. Bar, junk store, coffeehouse, diner. The sign in the junk store window reads MINI MALL.

Linus pulls in among SUVs painted the various colors of mud. He goes to the shop, he leans to the window. Racks and shelves. A thin light shows somewhere beyond but the room lies in dark. He tries the door. It jiggles but doesn't open. A cowbell attached to the knob inside clangs. He leans to the window again but no one comes, nothing moves.

He goes on. Past the shop's door and past the coffeehouse and the diner. He moves on past the line of shops around the brick corner and around a corner beyond that where he enters a dirt alley running the length of the block.

The light is different in this place. The sound is. He grinds earth under one foot. The noise of that grinding is profound and alone. Linus steps into the shadow. Graffiti made pale by years runs along old brick like cave art left by ancients. Alcoves open in places, bays for stock or for garbage. Doors textured dark. Linus passes each in slow walk. Only shadow, only footfalls and quiet. He counts shops as each goes by but there is no need.

The coupe is there waiting. Its turquoise skin stands luminous in the dim, immune to light's waning. He steps near and he touches the hood as if to make certain its presence, as if the coupe may be a ghost or a dream. The hood remains warm from the car's last driving. A print stays behind when he takes back his hand, dew slowly fading. He turns from the car.

The door is a darker patch in the gloom, not a door but the suggestion of a door. Maybe not a door at all but a hollow, a void leading inward to some cavern in the earth. Linus stares. He waits for something to emerge.

There is a clap somewhere, not here, a trashcan lid slamming down. Linus flinches, he gasps. He looks up the alley and down but nothing moves here. In three minutes' time he is back at his car.

The lights are on in the paper's lobby. A front desk kiosk stands empty but the desktop remains cluttered with worktime trifles. Computer and tablet, pens, remotes. A screen shows its waiting life. Stars shooting.

Linus passes beyond this unmanned post and he moves among a gathering of halls, some dark, some not. He rounds corners, circling deeper. When he comes to a light in an open door he enters and stands. A lamp lights an office. The nameplate reads Lawrence Harvey. In the corner there sits a bar cart decked with glasses, bottles. Linus pours a drink and he sips and wanders.

Trophies in frames show another world. Black and white faces captured smiling or stern. Captions recall small glories of the day. A strike, a founding. Moments. The man preserved is named August Kaminski in splashes of flavor text below each photo. The paper's owner, once upon when. Winner of this and that. Some other life.

A wristwatch sits on the desk. A thing left behind. Its dials finetuned go on tick, tick, ticking off seconds. Linus picks it up and he tries it on, he turns it around in the light. He shakes it from his wrist and sets it back on the desk. The dials go on ticking, no matter what.

His footsteps clack on the tile. The noise echoes along tangled hallways. The sound of a voice somewhere comes. Other clacking feet. Phantoms wandering somewhere inside the walls.

Linus moves in and out of the dark. Every other fixture is unlit. He travels tunneled corridors passing offices and break rooms, rooms lined with boxes stacked, rooms filled with nothing, their instruments dragged away, cords left trailing, spilled.

A door opens onto a space unlike the offices, the halls. This place too is left in dark. Sound falls away in a sense of deep void. The claps of each step touch faroff walls. Above the curving bulk of machine bones loom. Great engines stilled, the works of a gone people. Old scents hang cold on a breath. Ink and paper, oil and metal. Here and there a thin light shows. The dim presence of shrugged bulbs waiting. Gears and gauges affirming some halted desire. Things with claws and teeth.

More halls now. These walkways all look the same. He moves through and down and he turns in at a doorway and here he sits on a cot. The room is furnished with pulled scraps and nothing. Piled clothes, a lamp. Token necessaries. An ancient typewriter sits in one corner.

A canvas handle juts from a pile. He pulls and he drags and a bundle comes loose. Messenger bag. From this he takes a laptop. It comes to life in soft whirring. Linus stares at the screen. Its glow redrawing his face in skeletal pale. His eyes are gems in socket gloom, their glint shifting as they read.

Research. First the coupe man. Jeremy Red. Not much there. Business records, tax filings, all in good standing. No arrests, no headlines. Nothing, nothing. The search widens. Another man in town named Red died years back, decades back. Shot in a bank, a bystander in a robbery. Delbert Clayton Red. DC. A relative maybe. Linus notes it all down. He goes back to the missing man. Calvin Lond. Headlines are all the same. They know what they know, the man is gone. He clicks on each headline anyway. Another and another. And there it is. One thing has slipped through. He sits forward, he reads it again. A detail mentioned once and moved on from. The cops found the missing man's car.

He touches his face, he shakes his head. He closes the laptop and the room goes dark. He lies there, thinking. The world goes on. Somewhere a rolling drag of sound erupts like a garage door going up and then it stops and stays quiet. Clacks and humming talk come near too and in time they drift on, and he lies in dark stillness imagining where a man goes when he disappears.

2. The Car

He can hear the waters through trees. Their passing plays along rocks and shores like the notes of an old song. The cries of birds call down from their place among the branches, issuing opinion or protest not heeded or understood. Linus leaves his car at the road in what the photo shows to be the spot. This is where Calvin Lond's vehicle was found.

Cyclists. A dozen, two dozen. Helmeted spirits in breathable skins pedal their way through a backroad route whose meandering carries them twice each week past this frontier locale. The stretch of road stood bucolic and desolate as ever on the swarm's Wednesday passing, but when again they biked through the next Sunday there sat the luxury machine, windows down, keys on seat.

From that spot Linus leaves the road. He passes through the same ditch of high grass as did parties of searchers across weeks with nothing to show for all their efforts. He comes to the same rusting fence and he parts and passes between the same lines of wire. From here he walks toward the sound of water, following no trail but the one laid out by that melodic call.

Trees grow down to the shoreline. He steps over rocks and fallen limbs and when he reaches water's edge he stops. The world shimmers on the surface. The sound here is both loud and quiet, like a whisper hissed. He stands listening for some time.

When he moves he follows the water. Shoes sink into mud or they slip along rocks. In places he grabs onto low branches to maintain his step. The river's progression goes on around a curve stretched and subtle and maybe imagined, an illusion created by the lean of trees, some over water, some away. In time they peel back on this side of the river and a bridge of old iron does appear. Linus stands watching, as if waiting for something to happen. Planks are warped or they are missing and rods at angles have bent and in places snapped loose. The river moves and the wind stirs trees and grasses but beyond these the world has chosen to still. The birds if they are still there in the trembling verdure do not sing or speak. Linus steps onto the bridge.

Footfalls return a thick slap with each stride. Wood dry with years in the sun passes under his progression along the bridge to river's middle. Waters froth and churn and move onward as they forever have. Linus looks down, he looks into their testimony. The river is an organism both moving and standing still, a creature undefined, twisting and reaching and writhing within borders it has not chosen, unable now to break from its bonds but wearing at them, tearing away over long years so that unnoticed it may plot a new course.

When Linus thinks back to this moment he will not have a series of events to lay out in any lucid array, no order of things. The memory is a frayed chaos whose pieces are gathered between the reliable ends of linear time. He is looking down into the water's froth and then he is choking and no end is up in the world and he is speaking, he is screaming, but there is no sound emanating from him and all the sound there is is shapeless pressure in his ears as the world screams back, squeezing, squeezing, and his feet are touching something, and he is standing, his face touches air.

That first breath isn't a breath but a cough, and maybe it isn't that. He crawls and vomits water. His eyes are closed. He sits on knees and leans on hands. He takes in air, he lets it out. Body shakes with each breath. He stays in this pose for some time.

"Hello there."

Linus opens his eyes. In the grass beyond the river's wash there stands a block of stone running several feet to each side and on this block sits a man bearded and unkempt with one leg thrown across the knee of the other and at the ends of those legs shrouded in worn and mended trousers there dangle still fine oxfords.

Linus gets his feet under him. Clothes are twisted and bunched and his body drips water. Muck stains knees. He turns in a circle and stops. The transient watches Linus.

"Which way is the road?"

"Which road?" says the transient.

Linus looks left. He looks right. The trees grow thinner here, each a singular feature sprouting separate and alone among swaying grasses. The waters at his back have changed the direction of their flow since his time on the bridge. Linus follows their counsel. He looks back as he walks but the transient only sits at his perch on the stone watching.

Linus walks for some time. The way carries him around bends and through trees in their patches thickening and again thinning and it carries him up a rocky slope to a county road under which the river goes on its way. No traffic comes along. He turns and moves in the direction in which his loose understanding of these accumulated events dictates his car should be waiting. The scrape and shuffle of feet on gravel go on. His mind turns inward to recount the steps that led here, to mine them for value and meaning. The walking becomes a blur, a mechanical undertaking. He asks himself what a journalist would do but there is no answer. He goes on walking.

The road is empty for long minutes and then it is not as Linus' car comes into view. It waits there by the roadside where he left it. He squints, he leans. His feet renew their onward progress. The car nears. Beyond it the 1940 coupe with its whitewalls and flair sits parked. The coupe's window is down. Pale fingers tap. Linus stops alongside. That milk-white face turns his way.

"Hello, reporter."

Linus stands dripping. A puddle spreads on the pavement. The pale man looks him over.

"What happened to you?"

"I fell."

And.

"Are you following me?"

The pale man says nothing.

"Are you Jeremy Red?"

Nothing.

"I looked you up. The car."

"What are you after, reporter?"

Linus looks at the coupe and at the fence and the trees beyond the fence.

"This is where they found his car."

The pale man nods.

"I know."

The man starts the coupe up.

"You be safe out here," he says.

He pats the coupe's side with a pale hand as he pulls off down the winding back road.

————

His clothes slap as he walks. He's dried some but he is not dry. Mud flakes off in places. Little patches left on the floor.

He steps to a desk left vacant. A little tube TV plays the news. Muted visuals flipping. Hubbub of some kind. A big moment, it'll all change from here. A man in a wide tie talking and talking. Linus watches and waits.

A blue uniformed man stops along. Broad and gray and smiling. He says are you being helped and Linus says no and the man responds oh. He touches a button that coughs in another room. Can you help up here? We need somebody up here.

"We'll get you fixed up in a minute."

"Thank you."

The cop looks Linus up and down.

"You're all wet."

"I fell in the river."

"Is that why you're here?"

"I don't think so."

"Well," says the cop. "Good luck anyway."

The cop goes and a minute goes by and then comes a woman, older and small and round, hair in a pony. She smells like strawberries and she says hello, hello, are you being helped. Linus shakes his head.

"What can we do?"

"I'm trying to track down a car."

"Okay, good. What car are we looking for?"

"The Lond car? Calvin Lond?"

"Calvin Lond."

"The missing man."

"Okay. Oh. You'll have to check with impound."

"Where is impound?"

"Okay. You drive to the edge of town and stop. Turn right and go till you come to a bunch of cars in a field. Some will be behind a fence. You're at impound."

"They have the Lond car?"

"Hon, they might."

———

The field goes on forever. Off behind a long country road leading out away from town the rows of old cars are dumped in lines denoting eras like the rings of a tree, like the sediment deposits left trapped for all time in the wall of a cliff. Razor wire tops a chain link fence encircling a section paved alongside a little dirt road that cuts through the rusting shells and leading to an outbuilding. A cabin or shed. Linus pulls in. There is no slotted parking, no sign showing which cars are abandoned and which are not. He parks among the wreckage.

He steps into dust. No one comes, no one calls. He crosses to the shed and circles to a side that has a window with tin shutter pulled low and a door whose paint has long since peeled away. He knocks.

"Hello."

The voice that comes back from the little building says I'm coming, I'm coming. The shutter raises up in hitches and starts and behind it there is a man. Thick glasses, three-day beard. His dress shirt is yellowed in places, sleeves rolled above elbows. He leans forward into the now open space, harried.

"Yes?"

"A police clerk said I should talk to you."

The harried man waits for more. Then.

"Yes?"

"The Calvin Lond car."

A sound rolls in the harried man's chest. A word or a growl. He drags a tablet across the window's ledge and touches and touches and stares. Eyes darting over the screen.

"Auctioned off."

"What?"

"They auctioned. It off."

"Who did?"

"The county. They move quick."

"Don't the police need it for the investigation?"

"What investigation? This one came from a gone man. The cops zip some lights around inside, they hoover up a few spots if anything looks like anything, then they shuttle the thing off to be sold. Auctions do not wait."

"Can you tell me who bought it?"

"Of course not. I can give them your name. If they contact again."

"Do you think they will?"

"Probably not."

And.

"Hey. Hey. That car's gone. Don't be caught up on this. There are cars all around you. Anything you want is here to be had."

He gestures out at the field of forms dented and broken, skeletons from every age, the last decaying remains of storied frames going back and back into oldest lanes where rest the brittle parts of carriages cast off and left to rot here these one hundred years.

3. Stories and Gossip

He checks again, just in case. The address, the name, all. He's been there already but it doesn't matter. He checks. Mini Mall. Jeremy Red. He pulls the door and the cowbell clanks and the door opens for him to come.

The smell of smoke is there, a million cigarettes through the years. Ahead racks of nonsense baubles lead on. Dishes, toys. These shelves reach to head height or they reach to high ceiling and there is no clear order to their placement or to the items arranged along their tracks. A box holds all manner of watch and another is filled with old coins sheathed in protective casings. Tintype photos are left in piles here and there. One corner is stacked deep with paintings, their canvases facedown.

He moves among the shelves. Somewhere a radio talks and talks. A tinny announcer calls a game. Balls, strikes. The static buzz of crowd cheer. Still beyond this more, somewhere noise in another room, bings and bongs, bells. Infinite repetition. Now and then a woo or a hoot, hot damn.

He clears the stacks and there is a man there at a table. A suit in not silver but close. Shined fabric, synthetic. A cowboy hat sits on the tabletop, the brim too large and odd. The man looks up. He holds up a finger. Wait. The radio goes on calling. A hit, a run. The man is nodding. He looks up again.

"Can you even believe?"

Linus is nodding too.

"I guess I can't."

"I bet on em, can you believe it? A fool, a fool."

"I don't mean to interrupt."

The man gives a slight nod.

"Please. I got what I needed."

"Well. I'm looking for Jeremy Red."

The man in the silver suit sits back in his chair.

"Huh."

"What?"

"And who are you?"

"Is Mister Red around?"

"Okay, let's go with that. I'm Jeremy Red."

Linus shakes his head.

"Then who is the pale man?"

"Dutch?"

"He was in the coupe."

"The Dutchman works for me. My driver."

"You don't drive?"

"And who are you?" he asks again.

"I met him at the yard sale. At Calvin Lond's estate sale."

"Ah. The reporter. You're writing a book."

"Not a book. The Courant."

"The paper? In this town? Harvey must be thrilled."

Linus says nothing.

"Oh. Did Harvey send you to see me?"

Nothing. Red looks him over.

"Naw. Harvey didn't send you. You're a scrawny thing."

The silver suit man stands from the table. Jeremy Red. He leans and reaches and he puts on the hat. He says I'll make you a deal.

"I'm on my way to lunch at Caulder's. You have until my food comes to ask me your questions. After that you will kindly go away."

Linus agrees and he follows, out the door, down the block. They push through a door. The world inside is a diner. Salt and grease on the air. They sit down among cow bones and license plates nailed to walls. The table is shaped like driftwood. 3D printed maybe. A waitress appears and she smiles and lays down menus. Blond hair poofed with spray. She takes Jeremy Red's order, meat and potatoes. She turns to Linus and she says what would you like and he's speaking, he's ordering eggs, and Jeremy Red is saying oh, he says nothing for him, thanks. The waitress takes up the menus. She gives Linus a wink, she says be right out. Red lays his hat on the table.

"So. You have questions."

"Your driver was at Lond's house."

"Is that a question?"

"He took something."

Red waves a hand.

"Payment owed."

"Payment."

"I hired the man to do a job. Then he went and vanished. Fool that I am, I paid Lond up front."

"What was it you hired him to do?"

"Find a gun. No. Procure a gun."

"A gun."

"Yes."

"You can't get a gun?"

"Not this gun. Colt 1911. Used in a robbery. A lifetime ago now."

Linus takes out a notepad and pen. He looks and nods and writes.

"Why this gun?"

"It was used to kill my grandfather."

"Oh."

"Oh?"

"Delbert."

Jeremy Red straightens. A hand taps at the table.

"DC. Yes."

"Who has it?"

"The gun?"

Linus nods.

"You know that little museum on the highway?"

Linus shakes his head.

"The train car?"

Shrug.

"It's in there. Alton Everett has it."

"He runs the museum?"

"He killed my grandfather."

The pen stills. Linus lays it down.

"Alton Everett has the gun."

Jeremy Red nods.

"He killed your grandfather with that gun."

"Yes."

"Why isn't he in jail?"

Jeremy Red nods.

"Yeah. Yes. Why isn't he?"

"Is he capable of violence?"

Nostrils widen. Almost a laugh.

"My grandfather would say yes."

"I mean now. He must be old."

"What does this have to do with Lond? Why are you asking me this?"

"Well. You sent Lond to get the gun from him. If he didn't like it, if he was somebody who might see violence as the shortest answer for a problem that turns up. You know."

"Okay, sure. If Lond pressed him, that could happen."

Linus writes and writes. Then Red is speaking, he is saying you know he was robbing a bank. Everett was. Maybe shooting somebody was an accident, but you don't rob a bank without meaning to.

"Was Everett questioned?"

"Your paper covered it all. You shouldn't be bothering me. Lawrence Harvey used to be a reporter, if you can believe it. Back when the Pole owned the paper."

"Harvey reported on the robbery?"

"Go and ask him. It was a real paper then. An institution. He was the son of a bootlegger and half a moron but he was a good man."

"Harvey was?"

"The Pole was."

The waitress reappears. A tray and a plate steaming. Linus tries to speak but Jeremy Red shows a hard stare.

"Our deal is concluded. Be gone, reporter."

The waitress is going and Linus follows behind, he says hey, hey. She stops.

"Does that man come in here a lot?"

"A fair amount."

"What does he do?"

"He works down the block. The secondhand shop."

"That's it?"

She gives a huff.

"Oh he's harmless. He gambles some but he's no trouble."

He nods, he says thank you. He asks her name and she gives it, and he gives her his name, he goes to shake her hand. As they shake she says hang on just a minute, hang on, I got you some eggs to go.

———

He stops again at the strawberry clerk's desk. The tube TV, the flipping image. An anchor on the screen goes on about something on the way, some marvelous event yet to come. Linus watches and he is watching still when the clerk appears. Short and round and smelling of strawberries. She says hello and he says hello and she says okay.

"You found the car?"

"What?"

"You were looking for the Lond car."

"Oh. No. It was gone when I got there."

"Well shoot."

Linus nods. He presses close, leaning on the counter. He asks after Lawrence Harvey. Where is he held, how is he charged. The strawberry clerk nods. She says oh he's here. Down the block, kept at admin.

"There's a bit of a cluster eff."

Linus nods again. He asks if she can tell him the way, and she says okay, oh yes, okay. Down the block, the brick tower.

Out and down and on. Sidewalk traffic moves. He makes his way along. The building is there, the shaped facade of an old fort. Linus pushes through the door.

A sprawling lobby waits. Couches, chairs, space. Signs imply worlds contained, suites numbered and labeled with this thing, that thing. Lawyers, archives, more.

Linus comes to an elevator. A man sits with a key. Large and square build. Monitors glow on a desk before him. Linus begins to explain but the man says she called ahead, he says they'll be waiting, go on up. He inserts the key in a panel and nods. Walls chug with a coming. He waits. The square man looks at nothing. Waiting too. The doors are opening and Linus is entering and the square man is saying good luck.

An old song plays, or the idea of it. Melody familiar but not quite right, a jingle alteration of something known, revised into perversion. Then a bell dings and the doors open and ahead a long room waits. Tables like a cafeteria. Linus comes on, he picks one and sits. There is time. Time enough for nerves. Fingers tapping, heels bouncing.

Then.

An opposite door parts. The man who comes on is small, he is smiling. His suit is older, out of fashion some years. Too loose and fraying. He comes and he sits and waits. A small man. Pools of dark under eyes. Thin hair combed and parted with a severity. He leans. Hands clasp together. He waits.

"You're not handcuffed."

"I can't leave either," says the small man. "Purgatory."

"Well."

The small man nods. He waits. The commanding air of an executive comes rolling. He breathes in and out, he waits. Linus speaks up.

"Mr. Harvey. There are some questions. Maybe you can help."

"My lawyer isn't here."

"It's not about that. Not about your case. You covered a bank robbery for the paper years ago. A man was killed."

Harvey snorts.

"Years ago? Decades. Before you were born."

"Delbert Red was shot."

"I remember."

"What can you tell me about the guy they got for it?"

"For starters, they didn't."

"Didn't what?"

"You're talking about Alton Everett."

Linus says yes.

"The investigation labeled Everett a witness, no charges were ever brought. Not for Delbert Red and not for the robbery."

"But he did it."

"He says he did."

"You think he didn't?"

The man waits, smiling.

"How did he pull that off?"

Harvey shrugs. He says luck, more or less. A half dozen witnesses couldn't agree on a thing. Everett and

Red were in on it together, or they weren't, or it was an accident, it wasn't a robbery at all. Something else. Gossip, stories. He shrugs again.

"Cops stayed on him, then eventually they went on to the next thing."

"Do you know their names?"

"Who?"

"The cops."

Harvey shakes his head.

"Some old men. This was a lifetime ago."

Linus takes out his notepad. He asks if you mind and Harvey gives a slight nod, go ahead. Linus turns a page. The pen moves and moves and then Harvey is speaking, he is saying what is this, what is this about. He's saying who cares about the robbery now.

"There's a missing person. Alton Everett is supposed to be the last guy to see him."

"He didn't do it."

"Why do you say that?"

"Everett was small time, and now he's too old even for that. He was a conman more than he was a crook, and he was never a tough guy. He makes his living telling made-up versions of glory days stories to highway tourists who he sells overpriced t-shirts with the town logo. He's not the disappearing someone type."

"You don't think he's violent."

"I don't think it would occur to him. He would talk his way out of a situation before he'd go that way."

Linus writes in his notebook. He is still writing as he speaks.

"Which bank was it?"

"It's not there anymore. Oriel River Bank. River Suites now. It's a mixed use building. Apartments and offices just off downtown."

Linus writes. Then.

"What do you think happened? In the bank."

"Are you really asking?"

Linus nods. Harvey's breath comes slow.

"Not a robbery. Something else. Something that went bad."

Linus nods again. He writes in his notepad. He mutters and nods and speaks up.

"What about the gun?"

"What about it?"

"How did he get it back after the bank?"

"Man," says Lawrence Harvey. "You think that's really the same gun?"

———

The laptop gives off heat in the little room. A closet, a cubby. He sits on his cot and he clicks and reads. Eyes darting. There is nothing, nothing. No news of Lond, no ancient robberies. Headlines speak of some great moment just around the corner, invisible from here.

There is a clacking. Footsteps, a single set. Linus listens. He closes his eyes. They come on and they near and as they come along outside the door to this little nook they now stop. Now there is silence, now there is nothing. Seconds, longer. Then the step is again moving, then it is altogether gone. Linus listens. In time he closes the laptop.

4. Alton Everett

It's raised off the ground, laid on poured concrete, a full foundation. A train car pulled off the line somewhere along the way, years back. Repainted with care, all the old logos unseen in lifetimes. Stairs go all the way up. A wooden deck crafted by a lay hand abuts the train's door with boards warped and uneven. There is no lot but only a patch of earth beaten by the coming and going of would-be pilgrims to this roadside curiosity.

Linus parks down the way. The vast lot of a truckstop, diesels coming and going. Weighing, gassing. He settles in to wait and watch. He's not keeping time but yet it goes. When he does see something it is a man stepping out of the train car. Turning and locking. He wears a swell coat, yellow and long, the skin of some dead thing. The man's beard is full white but trimmed, shaped with some care. Alton Everett.

The car is aged luxury. Gray. A model much sought fifteen years back, twenty. He enters and starts and sits. Adjusting, maybe checking a phone. Sitting. Tail lights flicker and then he is moving, he is away.

Linus slides in behind. Some distance back, just in case. The gray car moves onto the highway and runs along for miles and then pulls off into suburbs, grids stamped between city and town. Linus follows along.

When the gray lux parks he parks. He watches. Pulled between cars on the street. Everett gets out and moves up the walk and rings the bell. A man answers, shorts and shirt in the day's chill. The man stands rigid. Everett speaks. Quite calm. The man bows up, he gestures a stiff arm as he talks. Everett talks and there is a moment and then the man is lessened in place, deflated. Strings cut. Everett says more now but the man only nods. Everett returns to the car. Linus follows on.

It goes that way, another in the suburbs, one in the city, then off into countryside. Brighter greens blossom as the rest fall away. Concretes subdued here, encroached by eager grasslands.

Alton Everett turns into a drive. He pulls in through gates left open for years. Rusted in place and hanging. A path driven much before. Ruts well worn in landscape otherwise much overgrown. Beyond this lies the last rest of many. Rows and rows of the dead. The gray car is lost in the path between stones. Linus parks along outer pillars and long iron bar lattice. He gets out in the grass and walks.

The path is straight. Between pillars and through the gate and on. The gray car sits along here. Empty and off, engine ticking. Side trails open, wandering deeper into the rows. Plots are washed away in swaying grasses. Tops of stones protrude from the tall growth. Here and there the thicket has been cut back to clear away a plot, to show a name chiseled there. There he stands in the distance. Everett. He holds the yellow coat close around his aged frame. Linus stops in front of any grave. Watching.

A rumble swells in the distance. Noise bounces across every corner of the world but Everett does not turn, he does not look up. He stands before a slab looking down at one of these stones, lips moving, speaking, to himself, to the dead, to God. The rumble settles and idles and then shuts off and the world is aggressive in its quiet.

There is a moment of nothing moving in the world. Then Everett has finished whatever private words he's had to share. Prayer or promise. He's moving among the growth, zigzagging back on the long walk to the gray lux. Linus moves too, he walks and then jogs. Through lanes to where Everett had stood. The grave is a simple stone. The name carved there is Delbert Clayton Red.

All is still now. He is running back the way he came. Between the graves and down the dirt rut leading to the open gate he runs and slows and fast walks and then jogs again. Out through the gate and around.

There by his car the coupe waits. Full in the road, engine off. The space is too close to go between. He steps around to the coupe's driver side. There the pale man sits. His silent film face. He looks over at Linus and nods. The window comes down slow.

"Hello, reporter."

"Your boss said you're called Dutch."

The pale man nods once.

"You are following me."

Dutch shows a smile. Amused and a little solemn. He says you think you are someone worth following. He says it again. You think you are. No one is following you. You tell our stories, some version. You are a witness to our lives. Here and now. A witness.

A car passes through the rusted gate. The gray luxury turns onto the road. Linus is speaking but his words are lost. The coupe roars into life. Dutch leans and he speaks too but the words are eaten in the noise. Then the coupe is pulling off into the road and away and on. Dust kicked up ahead in a mile of haze. Linus gets in his car and starts it up and follows along, he guns it along, but as he speeds ever on he finds only that drifting waft of just missed trespass, the engines of that sheen already long away.

———

He winds his way, hoping, trying. Back to town, all the way. It's pointless, they're gone. The gray lux, the coupe. He wanders still among varied city blocks inward toward downtown and then he is pulling over, he is pausing, not to think but to absorb, to be. The building alongside which he's parked shows a sign. River Suites. It is not a coincidence. He's decided, why not. It's here. It's been here all these years. He gets out of the car.

The front door slides clear like a supermarket entry. There is no doorman. The foyer is all blues and grays. A few chairs, a sofa. Some plants scattered. An island in the middle. The shape of a bank remains.

A hallway goes on. Black and white check flooring, faux vintage. Doors lead off to the worlds they contain. Homes, workspaces. Numbers label each without clarity.

Linus proceeds. All here is silent. No warble of television noise, no low thump of song. The clatter of little moments is stilled. He turns corners and follows hallways and ahead there lies an oddity. A hall ends in a vault door. He comes near. A steel wheel stands out. He touches it, he turns it. A dial ticks inside. He places one hand flat on the old steel door. A coolness there. He turns back.

Around hallways and down. When he finds a door with no number he knocks. Office. There is some wait. The door comes open and a man is there standing. Short and slender and dressed rather well, the suit of the help but cut sharp, stitched with a fineness. Slick hair combed back, the face of a man of any age. Old thirty, young sixty.

"Can I help you?"

"Are you the building manager?"

"I am."

"I just had a couple questions."

"About a space?"

"About the bank."

The well dressed man stands. He sucks his own teeth, a loud sound in the silence. He waves Linus on. Words are mumbled; tea, lease, come, come. Linus follows the man.

The space beyond is humble. A foyer of sorts. Table and chairs. The well dressed man says hang on. He steps out through a doorway and he mumbles some more. Linus sits. He shifts in place. Listening and trying to hear. The well dressed man returns. He sits with a primness. He sets down two teacups, handles turned just so. Teabags with strings hang over cup sides. He retrieves a cup, he holds it in two hands.

"Are you police?"

Linus shakes his head.

"Journalist."

"Interesting," says the well dressed man, and he says it again. "Interesting."

And.

"You have questions."

"This bank was robbed."

"Robbed, yes. Attempted, at least."

"Do you know the story?"

"Only as gossip. Gosh. I know there's a story. That was so long ago."

"People talk."

The well dressed man sips his tea.

"Someone's been asking," he says.

"About the bank?"

"About the robbery."

"Who's been asking?"

"A man. I don't know."

"What did you tell him?"

"What could I? It's all been said. Anyone who was there has said what they're going to. All the young men are old and all the old men are dead. Thankfully I remain vital, and thus, I have nothing to say that they haven't already."

Linus laughs and puts a hand on the teacup. The well dressed man watches. Linus does not drink.

"I have another question."

"Uh huh."

"The vault."

"Yes?"

"Why is it still back there?"

Eyes roll. He sips his tea. Then.

"That's long before my time, but it would cost too much to have it removed, so the story goes."

"What's inside?"

"That depends entirely on who you ask. The owner says it's full of a whole lot of dust and nothing. But people talk. They say the gangster who used to run the paper was using the place as his private bank. They say somebody he got sideways with locked him in there way back when."

"Couldn't the current owner just open it up and dispel the gossip?"

"People love a legend. What's that worth? Besides, alas, somewhere along the way the combination's been lost to time. So the story goes."

5. A Fight

The radio is a mumble now. Going on about who knows what, too low to hear. The bings and bongs are there still, the noise of some other room. The smoke and drifting cigarette haze.

Jeremy Red looks up as Linus clears the stacks. A smile spreads on his face. Hey, he says. The word is strung along. Heeeeey.

"Reporter's come back."

He turns a dial and the radio chatter falls away. A hand points palm up. Sit. Linus does.

"I ran into your man a few times. Dutch."

"How odd. What were you doing?"

"Asking around. About Alton Everett and what happened."

"What happened."

"The bank."

"You're investigating the bank now?"

Linus shrugs.

"I just have a few questions."

"I don't doubt it, but you've also got some kind of timing."

"What does that mean?"

"Would you believe it, we're on our way out."

"It'll just take a minute."

Somewhere a voice whoops. Bells ring. Jeremy Red rises. He takes up his overlarge hat, he pats it on a thigh.

"Tell you what. You want something for your book. You ever been to a fight?"

"What kind of fight?"

"Any kind."

"No."

"Reporter. Oh reporter. Come along. Have yourself a night."

"You'll answer my questions?"

"Ride along with me. We can talk on the way."

He swats the hat against a leg, once, twice. Without more talk he turns. The hallway beyond is a dark line. His form dissolves within. Linus pursues at a trot. The clangs of bells and the rest do grow. Doorways open onto rows of yanked slots, tokens dropped in machines by degrees of shriveled patrons. One room and then another. Then he is past and there is a deep metal clang and a back door opens onto waning daylight.

"It's open. Sit while we wait."

Jeremy Red points at the car. The coupe. He opens the back door and climbs in and he leaves it open for Linus to climb in too. Seconds fall by. He gestures at the console ahead.

"Well turn it on."

Linus reaches between the seats. He turns the key and the coupe roars a fury and then calms and waits. A modern screen alights tucked in the console. A song plays at first as thin noise and then as a richer tune that touches a vague emotional cord like the loose memory of some dream. Steel guitars and twang. He falls back into the seat.

"Now's your chance."

Linus nods.

"Your driver. Is he looking for Lond too?"

Jeremy Red waves a hand.

"What he's doing and what you're doing are not one thing. Maybe it's fate. We're all on the same path now."

"What is it?"

"What he's doing?"

Linus nods. Jeremy Red leans into the seat. Old leather gives. He is quiet a moment. Then.

"You ever have a supernatural experience?"

"Meaning what?"

"Anything. A run-in with the uncanny. You saw a ghost. You had a dream that came true. You turn on the radio and the song in your head is playing. Whatever."

"Nothing like that."

"I have."

He folds one leg over the other. Then he begins to talk. To tell a story about a card game.

"The dealer was giving a look. All night, this guy. When it's winding down and the dealer takes me aside. He has all these questions. But I figure this is a game too and the guy's working, so I sit down and we talk. He starts turning over cards and giving each one a look like it means something, what card is there. He asks me about my family. My grandfather. Everybody knows the story."

The driver door opens. The talk halts and there is a moment. Dutch lowers into the seat. He looks in the mirror at Linus and he pulls the door shut and Jeremy Red speaks up.

"I need to make a stop on the way."

Dutch gives the slightest of nods and he looks on in the mirror a moment longer. Then he is shifting gears and the car is loosing its growl and they all begin to move. Jeremy Red is talking. Where was I, where was I.

"It goes on like that with the cards. And he turns one over, and he's staring at it a while, and then he gives me this look. I don't know what it means, but I don't like it. This guy slides the card over, and it isn't anything, a jack of I think clubs, and he says, would you like to ask him. And I say ask him what. My grandfather. He says, would you like to ask him what happened that day in the bank. How do you respond to something like that? I tell him I don't know, because I don't, I don't even know what that means. He says there's a place out in the desert. And he starts writing down numbers and names for places somewhere out there. Hours out. He says if you go here and you sit, you can ask him. You can sit with him and talk. I'm still asking questions here but he says you just go. You sit and you wait. If you wait long enough and he doesn't show up, maybe you take more drastic measures. More drastic. What he means is if my dead grandfather doesn't appear to me there in the desert, I go see him on his terms. I kill myself.

"Now I should say, we were drinking, me and the dealer. Everybody's gone, it's just us now. And I'm amused, I'm having a high time. But what he's saying starts to take on something. A weight, I don't know. It's fun and then it isn't. Now he's starting to worry me. Now I'm getting concerned. What is this? What's he trying to do? But he packs up his cards and he leaves me there thinking. Come the next day it doesn't seem real. But those directions are there. These notes. And the day after that I'm driving west. Off on a long straight road, me and a few trucks. I'm out there and I throw a rod, something."

"Not the coupe."

"Not the coupe."

"You were driving yourself."

"Driving myself. I check, and it's fucked, I can't fix it. I call somebody, a service. But I'm out there. Out there. I'm sitting on the pavement thinking. Watching a thousand cars go by. And I start to really look at what I'm doing. The absurdity of it. A man I don't know got me out there, stuck along the side of the road. And it starts to really get me, you know? Why does it matter? The past is just stories and gossip. And I'm laughing. Thinking about it all and laughing. The car service gets out there eventually and they find me sitting, waiting. By then it's been, I don't know. Hours. I've had the time, I've figured it out. I know what to do, whether it's what that card man intended or not. And you know what? I kind of think it was."

"What was?"

"I'm supposed to make it right. I'm gonna get that gun."

He trails off. Linus writes in his notebook. He turns a page and goes on writing. The coupe rounds a corner and rolls on and rounds another and parks. Jeremy Red steps from the car. He pulls on his hat and runs a hand down his suit front and he enters a storefront door. Now Linus is there in the car. Alone there with Dutch. The other man watches in the mirror, that gaze measuring.

"You got him talking."

"I had a few questions."

"You shouldn't be asking him about that."

"It's just some questions."

"You shouldn't be asking him."

He looks away now, those eyes in the mirror. His hand taps the screen, the stereo lit. He taps and taps until a song comes on singing a song rich and sad. Old. Trumpets, men in suits. He taps the song louder. Now he sits with eyes closed. Linus writes in his notebook.

Minutes pass. A song plays and then another. Old woe howled in every line. Then the door is pulled open and Jeremy Red falls into the seat. He pulls the door shut with a clap. Well. Let's go, he says. Turn that off, he says.

Dutch touches the screen. The song changes and changes until he turns away. Jeremy Red settles.

"He loves those lounge boys."

The twang again now. Not all that different from what came before. Red says turn it up and he does. They pull away. On through town and across and over the whoosh of interstate flow and on through loose settlements tucked away in trees or fenced and then for a time nothing. Red says you like this. Linus shifts. He says what. What. This song? Red nods. Something old plays. Forever back. The bare reaching finger of some noise. God knows. Another song. Another song. They go on. West and then south. Miles.

First they see the lights. The headlights of a dozen trucks, cars. Two dozen. More. Lamps set on hoods. Some yellow, some pale. They're parked in a field and they're parked in ditches along the road. The coupe pulls off among them. The engine stills and ticks. The men get out. All around moves the smell of sweat and fire. Linus follows Dutch through the throw of vehicles set at all angles and past the shapes of figures moving in the night and out into a field of what feels like tall grasses and the thin light of electric lamps in the grass or in the backs of pickups spread in a rough circle around a patch of dark, still night.

Linus turns in place. Shapes move in the dark and they whisper and laugh like wraiths conspiring. They talk of a goon and they talk of a farmer and they spout numbers, amounts, wagers. The noise of swigs from bottles now and then manifests in a satisfying glug. The disembodied embers of cigarettes bob in front of faces that appear only when the pull of hot breath stokes flame.

The merriment dies away as the prickling of some animal understanding flows among the gathered. Each body turns to the darkness, the place in that crude circle where no lamps are set and no embers move. There is a cough somewhere and a featureless rustling and then a man's voice is loosed in a boom.

"Welcome, all."

He speaks through a bullhorn. He gives a little speech. This man, that man. The crowd hums along. Then it is time.

Pop. A light comes on, a single harsh bulb at the top of a pole, washing perverse daylight into a world in which it does not belong. At the pole's foot stands a man in a cheap suit and round glasses with lenses shining a hard silver in that pale glare. The referee. At one end of that throw of light waits a man in worn jeans and a gray work shirt, hunched and staring out of a skull perched atop a trunk of neck. Across the field from this farmer there is a goon in thick slacks, a waistcoat over a shirt with sleeves rolled to elbows, old gloves resewn and patched. On his head is a bowler that he removes.

The farmer starts to move across the field under that light.

The goon sets his hat on the hood of a late model something and he takes off one glove and then the other and places these in the hat. He turns, he waits. The farmer reaches the goon and he swings and the referee is moving and the crowd is shouting and this goes on for some minutes and then without the ring of a bell or any sign to mark the change the two men do part and a first round has come to its end.

Linus looks around. Dutch is not here, Jeremy Red is not here. The referee is here and Linus says hello and the referee nods. He lights a cigarette with a metal lighter that even in the stink of gathered bodies can be smelled above the din, the sharp cut of fuel on the air like the oil of ancient lamps. He smokes the cigarette down to a nub and pats it out against the heel of a modest work shoe and puts the filter in a pant pocket. He lights another and steps back into the circle of light and chatter among the gathered ceases. The fighters come from somewhere offstage to again take their places. The referee raises a hand. Every body among them tenses. He swings that hand down. The goon begins to sprint. He crosses the open space at a hard run, and the farmer hesitates, his stance wavers under this advance, and then the goon is on him, he is leaping and he is wrapping his legs around the farmer's waist and punching and screaming a mad, high wail as he rains wild blows. He rides the farmer to the ground and he goes on punching and hollering and the farmer is shouting words no one can make out under the assault and then he rolls and the goon is shaken loose to come up on his feet and circle the other man. Words are exchanged between the two men but the voices do not carry and they are lost to all but the combatants. The farmer moves in slow steps around the field's pole with its center light and the goon orbits the farmer like some lunatic moon and as they together near the light's edge and with it the gathered with their loose array of conveyances the goon says in a calm, clear voice a word. Okay. And now he is jumping and his body is twisting and one hard punch connects with a meaty thump and then the farmer is turning and he is spinning downward and his face bounces off the tailgate of an ancient hauler.

The crowd gasps and some groan and then in a growing quiet someone says well that's done, and it is, it is done. Money begins changing hands with disappointed slaps. And there is the referee, and there is Jeremy Red. They lean and confer, and the referee nods, and he raises a shoe and mashes out a cigarette on its heel. He nods again at what is said.

Linus finds himself beside Dutch. He paws at the pale man and points.

"What are they saying?"

Somewhere there are more gasps. Some point, others only watch. The farmer is there among the crowd. His jaw is all wrong and his eyes jar in their impossible lucidity.

"That man needs to go to a hospital," says Dutch.

The truck rolls along. Old shocks bounce with a stiffness. The farmer holds a wad of gauze clinched between teeth. He looks around with such a clarity that haunts. Linus holds his messenger bag in his lap, quiet, present. Working. The referee leans across the wheel and holds to the road. Miles move fast now. Country and suburbs and city. Streets lit in sodium yellow. An omnipresent buzz.

They wind their way past a hospital complex and past corner docs of varied accommodations and when they do pull in it is out front of a gray and sparse office park. Windows lit at random, each floor winking.

The men file out of the truck. A moment to reflect. The farmer mumbles and points. Lots of nodding. The referee says yes, yes. Go on up.

Hushed talk. These men lean as on some issue they disagree. More pointing, more nodding. Shrugged assurance now. The farmer walks on through a set of doors waiting. They watch him go.

"You going in too?"

The referee shakes his head no.

"I don't like violence."

He sits in the open truck. Dual cab. Decals there on the door. The name of a roofer. Phone number. He lights up a cigarette.

"Red told me about your book."

Linus says nothing.

"There was another one."

"Another what?"

"A missing man. Something Digby. John maybe. He worked in politics, around politics. Locally. I did his sister's fence last spring. Nice lady."

"Did he know Alton Everett?"

"I don't know. I know they had a guy for it."

"Who?"

"I don't remember. Some guy."

"Did he do it?"

"Maybe. The cops fucked up some process thing and had to let him go. It was in the news. He's suing everybody sideways."

Linus stands thinking. Then.

"Do you remember the sister's name?"

The referee leans and puts the cigarette in his mouth where it hangs and he pats his jacket and brings from some inner pocket a battered ledger. Pages flip to the middle. He holds the ledger out for Linus to see. Linus looks and he writes and looks some more. He nods. The referee puts the ledger away. He smokes.

Linus drops the tailgate. He hops up and sits scrolling his phone. Searching. The sister. Angela Digby. A place out in the suburbs. Bland history, all the usual. Normal, all. The brother, the missing man. John Jeffrey Digby. Junior blue blood. They lived together, the siblings. Headlines and talk around his disappearance. It's in the news and then it isn't. People forget. They move on. He keeps looking. The accused. Peck Algers. No background, nothing. He does not exist before he is arrested. A phantom. He's suing the cops, he's suing the town. An email address is listed here and there in connection with Algers' lawsuits. Something esquire. Lawyers. Linus writes up a message, he sends it off, what the hell. He puts away the phone.

There is some waiting and nothing. Then the farmer is there at the door. Coming out. Around his face is wrapped some sort of apparatus. Foam, plastic. Like the headgear and mouth guard of a sparring boxer. He comes along to the truck. The referee claps his arm.

"Not looking so bad now."

The farmer hands over a bag. He scribbles in his own notepad. I NEED TO SEE A SURGEON PLEASE.

"Another doctor, he told you. Fuck him, he doesn't want the liability."

The farmer makes a sound, a moan.

"I'll get you there in the morning. It's too late tonight."

The referee digs through the bag. He upturns it into a hand. A pill bottle rolls out. He holds the label up in the light, he slides on spectacles hanging on a string.

"Good God. Did you take this?"

The farmer nods.

"Get in the truck."

The farmer gets in the back seat. Linus and the referee climb up front. There is a moment.

"Are you in any hurry?"

Linus says he is not.

"We're in it now. I may as well use the night. Nobody is gonna see him before sunup. Nobody I can get him in to."

"What did they give him?"

"A lot."

And.

"You play cards?"

Linus gives a shrug. He says he does play cards.

"Okay then."

The referee starts up the truck.

———

The world turns on an axis. City streets appear and reappear in some tacit pursuit. Streetlights twinkle like starshine above. Somehow nothing moves. The truck alone exists along these byzantine lanes.

They pull into a side lot. The sign out front is some man's name. Vaguely German. Booze signage hums in a window. The referee says wait here. He gets out and goes in and is gone for some minutes. When he returns he's shaking his head.

"No dice."

Onward. The path is divined by some arcane belief held by the referee alone. He does not speak, he does not explain. The farmer breathes heavy in the back seat. Linus watches the night.

The next stop is at some sort of complex. Apartment building, long. A box of so many lives. The referee stands out front talking to someone through a speaker. His hands move as he talks. Then a latch clicks and a door drifts open and he goes inside. Linus waits. He turns. The farmer is slumped in the back seat. Chest moving. Near a snore. Nothing moves outside. Night sounds exist in the stillness. The hint of a voice somewhere. Traffic some ways off. Disembodied machine hum. When the referee reappears he holds up thumbs. He gets in the truck and says good, okay, good.

"We've got us a game."

The pickup navigates streets lined with banal reproductions of clumped estates on a route winding inward like some suburban black hole. They pass by a hundred of the same house, and a hundred more, and then they are slowing, they are stopping at one like any other.

They're not the first to come. A gravel drive curves around the residence. All manner of make and model wait there. They pull in among the rest. The referee and Linus get out into quiet night. The farmer is left in the truck sleeping.

The referee goes to knock. There is a wait. A camera hangs from the canopy. A profound thump sounds within the door. The referee reaches and pulls it open.

A long vein of hallway lies ahead. The two men move along old wood floors that echo a rich tone with each footfall. Light from an open doorway brings them on. A man at the door steps aside. They are here.

One after another they enter a room in which a man sits at a table of plain wood dealing out cards to himself and other seated strangers and turning over this one or that in a game whose rules only he has been made aware. He gathers these again and he says to the newcomers hello, and he says sit, sit, and he shuffles the deck. He deals cards and he asks them if they've played before and even if they have not they say they have. Money comes out and they bet and win and lose and keep going. The man from the door brings bottles and glasses and each man drinks. The dealer deals cards and he says he is something of a card player himself and at times a mystic as well and the men laugh all but the dealer. They drink and they bet. Money gathers in a pool and spills and shifts. Linus wins and loses and wins and wins. He wins and they clap him on the back and they drink. When Linus says he has to go to work the men boo and they laugh and one among them says you're at work now. They vow to keep playing. Someone calls Linus a car and he plays another round as he waits. He plays it through and wins again.

———

Morning sun dares to appear. They wind along the town's outskirts. Linus talking about missing men and a bank robbery. The driver eyeing in the rearview. Linus gets out down the street from the paper. He pats the car's roof as it goes.

The sun is dragged higher by moments. An onset relentless. Dawn traffic begins its rousing. Souls on their way to today. He makes his way in awkward step. And then.

Lights are swirling with a wildness. Blues, reds, more. The lot is full of them. Vans, trucks. Squads positioned in place. The newspaper is a swarm of cops. Still he approaches, he comes near. This is home.

It's a tableau. The light swirl, the rest. Men in odd plastic wraps carry boxes out to a trailer. Bubble outfits. Linus watches. He sits on a curb. Passing cars slow to look. Men come and go in their alien suits and then settle and for a time the movement reconciles and

Linus comes on. His car is there at lot's end waiting. He doesn't remember walking. He gets in and it starts up fine and none of the men in their plastic suits or the blue uniformed gorillas standing around smoking make any move to stop him.

6. The Suburbs and Another Missing Man

Linus sits alone in the diner among walls of faux rustic decor. He orders coffee and a small man brings it and he drinks it down and orders another. The room sweats away from outside winds. The scoured heads of long dead cattle looking down.

"Hello again."

The waitress is there. She's smiling at Linus.

"Out early or out late?"

Linus wags a hand.

"Have you eaten?"

He shrugs, he says he has not.

"Hang tight," she says. "Don't leave."

She's not gone long. When she comes she has a plate. Eggs piled high and steaming, toast just a little burned. She sets it down with coffee sloshing in a pot.

"Personal stash. Use it wisely."

Linus says thank you. He reaches into a pocket but she says it's gratis. He pulls from the pocket a wad of bills. She snorts.

"Well now it's not," she says.

He lays out cash and he says thank you again. He eats in slow plodding bites between drinks to wash it down. Morning crowd grows around him. The ting-aling of a bell. He goes on eating. A man watches from another table. Hollow eyes, shirt loose at the neck. He points at the coffee where it sits on the table and he says there's some law. About serving. Linus nods. The man at the other table says his name and Linus says his name and the man nods. He says nice to meet you. And.

"You see that plate there?"

He points at a corroded square of metal stamped with numbers and letters and hung among dozens of the same.

"That was my grandfather's car."

"What kind of car?"

"Old Ford. After the war."

"How did it get up there?"

"How does anything get anywhere? Somebody gave it or somebody took it."

"Which was it here?"

"Depends on who you ask."

The man goes on looking at the plate where it hangs. Linus says thank you but the man isn't listening. The waitress returns. She takes up the coffee pot and pours his cup full. Linus says thank you. He says he would've done it but there's some law.

"Are you waiting on someone?"

"I have someplace to be but I'm too tired."

"Get some sleep, man. What are you doing?"

Linus says nothing.

"Oh."

Linus says nothing.

"Hey. But. There's an apartment over the coffee place up the block. Let me talk to the guy on my break."

Linus says talk to him. He says thank you, he says please. He says I'll come back, I'll check back. She takes out a phone.

"What's your number? I'll text you?"

He says it again, I'll check back. He rises and trips away and a man is there passing by. Unkempt and frail of limb but his shoes are shined oxfords and on one thin wrist hangs the fine-tuned wristwatch of a man of wealth. Linus eyes the transient and the transient eyes Linus. Then he is through the door and out.

The morning is there. Pressing in, this existential shift change. He breathes. Air wafts along, somehow cool and cloying both before the onset of full day. He crosses to slanted spaces across from the line of storefronts and he moves to the car and falls into the back seat. He curls, he pulls the door shut at his feet. The late breakfast hour swells all around with cars that do come and go, and their riders enter shops or they leave or they stand around in this liminal space swapping human prattle in urgent voice. Linus dozes and rolls in a fever haze. Dreaming and not dreaming. Thinking and then slipping. Falling into some place open between places. Rolling still. Cold and hot in turn. Damp, wet. Clothes stick to skin. The voices still. Rising, falling, talking of today mundanity. Talk. The sun now. Could you believe it. Hats removed and handkerchiefs out to blow a nose or to dab away oppressive dayshine.

Linus is sitting up. He's gripping car seat, he is pulling, stretching. He checks his phone but there is nothing there but the time. No text, no email. He shifts and scoots out onto the day. The sun has moved so far.

He touches his face and he wipes it, presses it. He moves around to sit behind the wheel. Thinking. He checks the phone again. He huffs. He pulls the notebook and flips pages and taps in the sister's info. He pulls the door shut. He pushes it out and claps it shut again just in case.

There is a kind of jam. Cars going and coming. Someone honks. Linus waits. A car cruises on by. Vintage and long, a box the color of old blood. It rolls slow as it goes. Linus pulls out next and he joins the flow as it draws their progression along.

———

That computer voice commands. It chimes in all along. Turn, go. That voice directs the way on. Suburbs coalesce, details hardening with such intimate nearness. Streets named for trees cut down in a different world. There is a turn into a neighborhood circle and here he pulls the car over and parks. Binging computer voice. You have arrived.

Too much sits here. Perched. Unmoving, waiting. He steps out onto patched macadam. Quiet porches and driveways and patios all around. One lot empty but for a broken slab where a house once stood. He turns and turns again. There on a porch a dog and on second look too a bird. He nods, he waves but so what. He walks up a drive.

The bell thumps deep in walls. Then the wait. When she opens she steps out proud, strong. Hair falls long, streaked in gray. Linus is polite, he backs away. She gives him space. They talk and she gives him more space. He explains. The story, a man missing, all. She says she will bring tea but she does not invite him in.

He finds himself sitting. Old wood rockers here. He waits with little rocking. The quiet town. A car somewhere comes or goes. The lightest brush of the sound of it. Then.

"I'd like to not press it. The wound's still there."

She steps onto the porch with a tray. Cups, the rest. She sits with the thought.

"Though if I'm being honest, there's not a whole lot to press."

"Can I ask some questions?"

She shrugs, she says sure. He says your brother and already she breathes heavy. Cup in hand.

"My brother."

"Do you have thoughts?"

"Of course I have thoughts. Young man. I have nothing but thoughts.

"I'm sorry. Hey."

A silence swells. Awkward. He turns and turns away and turns back.

"Just a few questions. I'm sorry."

And she is nodding, and she is saying fine, fine.

"Did your brother know a man named Alton Everett?"

"Who is he?"

"He's nobody."

"Nobody nobody or nobody don't worry about it?"

"He's nobody. Probably nobody. What can you tell me about the guy they arrested for your thing?"

"Him. Peck Algers. He's angry. I don't know. He should be angry."

She sips her tea. Then.

"You're wondering if Algers did it. If he's responsible for my brother, and then maybe your missing man after that."

"Is he?"

"That poor man didn't hurt my brother. I hope he wins in court. After what they did."

Moments of quiet. She's watching the road but not really. Thoughts turning inward on toward the dark middle where all things go. She shakes her head a little. Linus sees. The moment breaks and she speaks.

"Tell me about your nobody."

"Alton Everett."

"Who is he?"

"I think he's a conman."

She gives him a look."

"What?"

"Peck Algers is a conman."

"You said he didn't deserve what he got."

"There are degrees."

"You think he's a conman."

She nods.

"Sometimes the world is small."

"Isn't it."

"You think it means something?"

She shrugs.

"Maybe not. Just. In my case it's plain as day a decision was made. Hanging some grifter for all the sins in the world was a less resistant path than finding out what really happened."

"There's a connection there."

"Sure there is. But somebody may want your nobody to be the guy for reasons other than him being the guy."

Linus nods. He sips his tea and he drinks the rest down. Somewhere in a pocket his phone gives a ping. He sets the teacup back among the fine set on its tray. He stands and leans and puts out a hand and she shakes it. She pats that hand with her other. Soft skin, gentle. She stands to see him go.

"Good luck with your nobody," she says.

———

He sits in the car for minutes. Eyes fall closed on their own. When they open the sky has changed. The sun is falling away. Pink splash tinged in bruise. He sits up straight, he takes out his phone. The email is there. He reads it again every word.

> Hello sir. What a pleasure. Your note is an inspiration. Come tonight at your earliest convenience, my office will be open.
>
> —Peck Algers, Esq

Below this an address. Warehouse district, deep in the city. Linus checks the time. The sun is almost gone.

———

The city's outcroppings swell and consume the territories. Paths narrow and towers reach heavenward.

Shapes stand in windows with boxed lies lit at their backs. Bricks wear viscous trails that glitter on building sides under feeble streetlamp glow.

Traffic glitters and shop windows show bright and the city is full of bodies moving along to wherever and without signal or sign these at once cease and the way ahead becomes long blocks of concrete which in daylight's fall would be filled with row after row of long haul trailers pulling all manner of good stopped here to load or unload or for drivers to nap or eat or pursue more lurid necessaries. Now there is nothing. Empty acres of lot out front of sheet metal faces or cement faces or other assemblages more arcane. Warehouses, barns, hangars. Older facilities boarded up, smokestacks falling. Some fenced, most not. Ghosts of industry long fled or here and there a thing reborn in some other function. The robot voice guides. A spell of its own kind whispering secrets. Drawing the listener on. In.

Linus crosses an open span. Pastures of asphalt. Yellow lined slots standing empty. Paint fading on broken ground. He pulls in at a dock numbered in a long line of identical bays. The robot voice has fallen quiet along with the world. He steps out in still night. A cat watches from a closed bay ledge. Tail switching. Linus nods. The cat remains.

Stairs lead to a door. A number pad is lit glowing. A button to talk. He presses and waits. Buzzing. Then the door hiccups and clicks and he pulls the way open.

The room beyond is a void. Reaching. The pull of dark seeks to crowd. Sound travels all wrong. Impossibly cavernous. Onward there is a square of light. He moves that way, there is nothing else. A window resolves. A door alongside. He opens and enters. An office. Spare, utilitarian. The bikini calendar of another year. In box out box empty. Framed photos of God knows who. Desk.

The man at the desk smiles. Peck Algers. He reaches, he points. Linus sits across.

"So nice now."

He nods at his own speaking. Before him a plate. Some sort of sandwich. He touches it in little pats.

"So. You're the man with questions."

"There's a man missing."

"The world is a well of mystery."

"I'm sorry to be of inconvenience."

"Friend. My friend. A leaf in a river does not hurt the flow. You are not harming me."

Linus says okay. He brings out a notepad and pen. He says okay again. Okay.

"I heard you got railroaded."

"The world is in need of answers, even when those answers are wrong."

Linus nods. He pokes at the notebook. Nodding still.

"Thank you for taking the time."

The man nods. Enthusiastic. He pushes forward a tray and lights up a cigarette and he mumbles half a word in smoke. A thought in drift bloom. Then he speaks again.

"It's not unfair."

"I haven't asked anything."

"Even still."

"Well. I have some questions."

"Are they bigger or smaller than the voice of the universe?"

"Well. I don't know."

The man makes a noise. He lays down his cigarette on the tray. A thin trail rising up still. He points at his sandwich and he dissects. A pickle removed. Linus watches. He speaks, he chimes in.

"Do you know Alton Everett?"

Algers shrugs. He pulls in the sandwich and bites and chews. He swallows and shrugs again.

"All men are known in this world or the next."

"What about Calvin Lond?"

Algers stops. He lays down the remains of the sandwich and stares.

"What are these names?"

"One is a missing man. The other is something else."

Algers turns his face away while his eyes stay on Linus. He turns it slow in the other direction. He smiles.

"What do you think?"

"About what?"

"The missing men?"

Linus shrugs.

"People disappear."

"Jesus Lord."

"Well. What should I think?"

"It is not for me to lead you. That is not the kind of understanding we have. There is evidence of luck or of God or something we cannot put a name to in the workings of these events. Do you not see them? Do you not feel their hands upon you? Name them as you wish but know them as their works draw near."

"So it's the work of God, these men disappearing."

"May as well be. I had nothing to do with it."

———

The heavens above are midnight dark. Linus pulls into an open slot across from the strip. The only car in the lot. He gets out and he crosses to the diner. All dark inside. The cow heads and the rest. Still he tries the door. Bolted for the night. He moves on.

The coffeehouse sign is unlit but a bulb glows behind the counter. He pulls this door too and the result is the same. He knocks on the window. Waiting.

A car pulls into the lot. Stopped along the curb. Headlights go out in a click. A square grill there. Body the color of old blood. The storefront jingles beside Linus.

"Yeah?"

A man stands in the open door. Dark hair poking out from a paper hat. A week's beard growth.

"I was told you have an apartment."

"Ah," says the man in the paper hat. "Oh."

The man steps back. He pulls the door wider. Linus comes on in. The man in the paper hat says you can give it a look. He points to a hallway off the main room as he says it. Linus asks how much and the man gives a number and Linus does not haggle. They trade talk of particulars and Linus again says okay and the two men shake hands. Linus leans down out of view and from the messenger bag he takes a wad of bills and peels off a selected few. This he hands over and the man says okay and their business is now complete.

Linus gathers his few things and carries them from the main room into the hall. A corridor goes off into the back with doors to bathrooms and an open access to the kitchen and next to this is a narrow set of stairs leading up. He follows this to the top where a door is standing open onto a small room. He enters, he shuts the door. The room is furnished with a small drawerless desk with a simple desk chair and an aged recliner the color of sand with its fabric worn thin in patches. A nook separated by a few feet of wall holds toilet, sink, a concrete shower stall. One uncurtained window looks out on the town's main drag. A mattress lays on the floor.

Linus sets down his things. He lowers his body into the recliner. He looks up at the ceiling and the sky beyond and he closes his eyes and goes on seeing, and leaning back in the chair he allows himself to sleep.

7. Pursuit!

First he hears the day. Cars passing, doors. Voices somewhere. The white noise of life. Scents waft from rooms below. Coffee, butter. Some kind of pastry. He rolls forward in the chair. Feet touch floor. He sits, eyes closed, breathing.

The way down is a wooden stairway. Impossibly narrow. He squeezes his way along, each step groaning, wood ancient now.

Lobby. Morning patrons chew donuts and bread treats slathered. They touch cards to a reader that boops, and a clerk slides over cups or a bag, and they all smile every one.

The counter man is the same. Dark hair, paper hat. Beard has grown by hours. He nods and he pushes across a Styrofoam cup and he does not ask for a card, he does not name a price.

"Can I get ice?"

"In that?"

"Please."

The counterman takes the cup back and with metal tongs he takes a few cubes from a long trough and drops them in. He pushes back the cup, and Linus sips, he says thank you. The counterman nods and they talk. The apartment, it's fine. It's fine. Little things here and there. It'll all work out. It's fine. Today's moving day.

The car chugs and then starts. He watches the mirror as he goes. Turns and turns just in case. No strange cars appear on the way.

The newspaper's lot is empty. He parks in the corner like always. No cars swarm, no one jumps out. Police tape drifts in gentle breeze. Torn and laying. Windows are broken here and there. He enters through the front door.

Desks are overturned like a bootlegger raid. Papers strewn. Tickertape party. Doors hang on broken hinges. Madness devoid of all purpose.

Corridors accept his presence. A familiarity coming. He makes his way to the room. Nothing there touched. He scoops clothes in a bag, and he digs, and he lifts, and he has what he's come for. He looks again just in case. The typewriter is there in its crate. He lifts the container up and he takes his varied things and he leaves this place for the last time.

———

He's ordered from who knows. Not her. Eggs come, and old coffee, and he's eating still as she steps near.

"Hungry then."

He nods, he says yes. She asks questions, she makes small talk. He nods, it's a long day. She nods. She goes to sit down.

"So," she says.

He flinches, he settles. She nods. He asks if she's hungry and she shrugs, she says sure, she says yeah. He waves over a waiter, some man, the small man, and he asks for eggs, coffee, more of the same. The waiter looks at the table and he looks at Linus and he nods and he goes. She speaks.

"The boys are talking."

Linus doesn't respond. She shrugs in the silence. She says they're talking about your book, and he doesn't correct her, and she asks him questions he doesn't have answers for, and he answers anyway. About Alton Everett, about Calvin Lond, others. Jeremy Red and the gun. Some of the names she knows, some of the faces.

The waiter comes with a plate and a cup, and for a time talk is changed. Eating and little quips and nods. Smiles. A television on a wall shows a man at a desk talking, making promises of wondrous days to come, none named, all vague. Hair impossibly quaffed. The two finish eating. She lays her utensils across the plate at parallels and sits leaning over the table.

"Can I help?" she says.

———

He's outside when her shift ends. She gets in and they go, across town, out along the service road alongside the highway to the same truckstop again. Another car among many coming and going. Men walk among the trucks, and women. Everyone working.

Linus watches the train car down the way. The waitress asks a question and he points. They talk a little and then they don't and there is a wait and now Alton Everett is out, he's locking up the roadside curiosity. That same coat, same put together frame. He gets in the gray car and goes. They follow along.

She's excited now. Hands patting thighs. She asks questions and he points. They don't leave town, turns wind around corners and down along humps of postwar alchemy and on into complexes of modern apartments going on for blocks and gated. The gray lux turns in at one among many. Everett punches in a code, and bars glide back on a rail, and he's gone.

There is a moment. Linus touches the gas, he eyes the slow way the gate crawls on back to true. Then it is closed and the moment is done.

She's looking at him, she's expecting a next step. Finally she asks.

"What now?"

He gives a nod toward nothing in particular.

"This," he says.

————

Ten minutes. Twenty. Then the gate clangs and parts in dry hitches. She makes a little noise and Linus says yes and they're off again. Still in town, downtown and through on to a long farm road that goes out of town and a long way besides. The gray lux stops short, pulling into a gravel lot at town's last edge out front of a set of shops built in some other world, planks nailed together by men dead these hundred years. More. Alton Everett gets out and goes in, a blank shape of a shack on the end slathered matte black, held together by layered paint and spite. A neon sign sizzles, some beer's name.

Linus parks across the street out front of what might once have been a hardware store and now is a frosted window of dust and nothing. He turns to the waitress and asks.

"You wanted to help."

She says yes. He says that man. Just go in. Just go see what he does inside.

"In there?"

Linus says in there.

"That's a knife fight bar."

"That's old men drinking in the dark. Nobody in there has been in a fight in fifty years."

"You promise?"

He says I'm right here. He says just look and come back. Hurry, hurry. She's out and she's going, inside, gone. Waiting again. He leans his head back. Almost pushing. More than almost. Fingers tap on the wheel. Grip the wheel. He's looking at the ceiling and he almost misses it. The coupe pulls up in the lot. Linus sits forward in his seat. He watches. Dutch gets out and he straightens the lines of a suit and he crosses the gravel lot to the bar's door and in. It's Linus now patting his thighs. The wait goes on, minutes and minutes. He mouths words to no one. Come on, come on. Then she is there, crossing the lot, crossing the street. Back in the car.

"He was there."

"Tell me everything."

"He got a drink and he talked to a bartender. About anything. Numbers. I don't know. Then he went in the back and came back, and he got into a thing with a guy. About a coat? He was really mad but the guy didn't seem to know what it was."

At that moment Dutch steps out into day. Linus sits up. He points.

"Is that the man he got into it with?"

She turns and looks and says no, no.

"That man didn't come near."

Linus slumps. Waiting. He says okay.

"Wait here."

"What are you doing?"

"I have to talk to that man."

He goes, and he's crossing the lot, he's coming near, and the coupe is there, the pale man is there. A cigarette hangs in one hand. Linus bows.

"What are you doing?"

"Mister Red doesn't like smoking in the car."

"No. Here. Are you following Everett?"

The pale man smiles. Ugly, mean.

"Mister Red told you."

"What did he tell me?"

"He wants that gun. He had an agreement."

Linus says sure. He mumbles nothing. Words, nodding. Help these days. On. Dutch breathes a cloud. Staring, measuring. He nods in places where there is nothing. He steps on the cigarette. Heel crushing. Not answering, never answering.

"How is he gonna get the gun now?"

But the pale man is looking past him now. Eyes hard, trailing. Linus turns, and Alton Everett is there, he is nodding as he passes by. Hello Dutch. He wears no coat now, a buttondown there, tailored, sleeves rolled. His eyes never touch Linus, and then he is gone. Soon then Dutch follows, into the coupe, into the street, away. Linus watches them go, one and then the other, shapes dwindling on into nothing. He is standing there still when the waitress comes to stand alongside.

"What did he say?"

Still he looks out at the street, the cars now gone, street empty, all things standing still.

"Red's gonna force the issue."

"What?"

Linus shakes his head.

"Let's go get a drink."

———

Streetlamps burn. The roads are all empty. Windows dark the whole way, the town sleeping. He pulls into the lot, a car among the few. A bread truck waiting for morning. A clunker waiting to be towed. One long box of a car the color of old blood. He says well and she says yeah and he says that was a day. He says it again, a long day, and she touches his hand. Do you want to come see the apartment? She nods, she says yes, and she does.

———

There is a bing. He sits up, he opens his eyes. The phone, the laptop, both. He pulls pants over and digs in pockets and the phone falls out, the screen lights. Email.

> Oh. Him. I had the pleasure of giving patronage to his roadside menagerie once. Though if I may be so bold, I suspect his income is not entirely on the level. So nice again to meet you. Bless.
>
> —Peck Algers, Esq.

At his side she stirs. A sound, a word maybe. He touches her calf and she settles. He shuts off the phone and lies back, and in the stillness of dark, night again comes.

8. Action

Linus wakes in a start. Alone now. A high sun pours in. Daytime noise comes as he rises and stands and waits for his bearings. Scents again. Coffee, sugar, more. He indulges in a number of breaths before dressing.

Nods and coffee and thank you and out. A waft of more day, too much almost. Then he is in the car and breathing again and he's off. The sun is so high. He shakes his face and lowers the window. Crossing town, wandering ever toward the town's busy fringe.

The highway is puttering. Sirens somewhere. Runoff congeals. Stop and go forward. The truckstop comes up, then the train car. There's no time to stop. Everett is out. He's in the lot shouting into a phone. Traffic is standing. The highway, the rest. He shoves the phone in a pocket, he folds into the gray lux. Enough traffic parts for him to become absorbed. Linus can only follow. The universe goes on moving.

Inching along for a mile, two. One lane standing stock still and then the other. Honking. At times cars veering off through grass to side streets and beyond. Then the gray lux is at an exit and he is pulling off the highway and then soon too Linus does the same.

Town winding. Shapes conform with an oddness. The contours of each place. Neighborhoods, settlements. Linus follows through these cutouts of places and Everett stops and Linus stops too.

Everett is out and up a walk. Prefab Tudor. Suburban nothing. A stasis. Squatted among bocks of these grotesques. Everett knocks and the door opens and he goes in. Linus waits. Time goes on. He closes his eyes. Still time goes.

———

The tap insists. Tack, tack, tack. He sucks in air. Awake now. The sun has moved. Going. Hours maybe.

Tack, tack, tack.

A man stands at the car window. Bone thin. Facial hair trimmed into lines, around the mouth and back. T-shirt worth a few hundred. A necklace shows a gem. He knocks with a ring.

Linus lowers the window.

"You waiting on something?"

"What?"

"You've been out here sitting."

"I was waiting for my friend."

"Your friend."

"He was parked here. Gray car."

And.

"I fell asleep."

The thin man's arms come up to hug himself. He stands staring.

"Your friend left."

"Do you know where he went?"

"You should go too."

"What was he here for?"

"I don't know you."

Linus leans down. The thin man steps away. When Linus rights he holds stacked bills. He slides one off the top and then one more. These he holds out. The man steps close again.

"I just want to know what he wanted."

The man hides away the bills.

"He came to make a friendly bet."

"You're a bookie."

"Goddamn, man. A friendly bet."

"Did you take it?"

The thin man says nothing.

"What was he betting on?"

The thin man shrugs. He says it again, I don't know you. His eyes glaze, shift down toward where the stack of bills might have gone. Linus says thank you. The window rolls up in fits.

———

The bar is just the same. A shack among shacks at the edge of town. A farm road running by and on into its country distant forever. Linus parks in the rocks. He walks to the door through long gravel drive. The whoosh of a passing car on occasion. Then comes the dark.

The entrance is misleading. Maybe from what remains of the sun. Light spilling through into that foyer. Then the door falls back in place and the truth of the dark is there. Only shapes now. Tables, a long bar top. Linus sits on a stool and he waits. The bartender is bent in talk with the hunched form of a patron at the bar. That someone nodding, nodding. Then a lurch of that form and a noise like a sob. The bartender reaches and speaks again. Patting. Then the moment is done and the bartender comes near.

"Drink?"

An older man. One eye milk, scarred. His mustache is wild grown. A week of beard beneath. Square build, hard even with years. Linus orders a drink. It comes and he sips. Time goes and the drink goes and he asks for another of the same. He sips and that one goes too.

The light comes at times. The door opening, closing. Men dragging along into the dark, only voices now ordering drinks and then sitting, quiet. Then it is different. Light and dark and Alton Everett comes through. He leans near to the bartender. They talk close. Everett reaches into a pocket and he brings out a fold. He begins counting out cash. The bartender touches his hand, he shakes his head. Everett insists. The bartender is staring, hard staring. He goes away and comes back. A ledger now. Scribbling. He takes Everett's money and that at once is gone and now Everett is smiling. He knocks once on the bar top. Then he goes. Light and dark and gone.

"How was that?"

The bartender turns his one good eye to Linus.

"What are you asking?"

"He seemed to have a bee in his bonnet."

"We weren't on the same page."

"You worked it out."

"He had the money to make it work."

Linus says hmm. He lays a few dollars on the bar and downs his drink and sets this on top of the money.

"Are you still taking bets?"
The bartender's one good eye goes dark.
"I don't know you."
Linus adds a dollar to the bar.

———

It's not gone. The gray lux. Linus gets in his car and waits and soon it's time, he is moving again. Everett first and then Linus. Out and following. Some ways behind. Crossing town again. Across the highway to fenced homestead plots in their country winding. The way is much the same. Twists and turns seen a time before. Still he follows, all the way. Pastures swallowing all. Paved road giving way to old stone and then dirt. Cloud kicking up behind.

Trailing. Taillights are there in the distance and then they are blinking and then they are gone, lost among the scattered reflection of a hundred more. The road is a throw of stopped cars. This side, that side. Linus pulls in with the rest. When his lights are gone the night is again a dense nothing. He steps out. The sounds of swaying mortals in the hundreds. Whispers and laughing. He whispers too. Nods but no one sees. Drifting in toward the center of what might come. This maze of bodies and cars. At a point they still. All these shifting pieces. Linus rests and waits. Watching the dark. Strangers gossip and lean. He's a hulk, I mean really. A monster man, can you even believe. Linus asks for a cigarette and a stranger says friend of course and Linus sits smoking in the night. Mechanical thumps. A microphone tap. Gathered, gathered. You've seen fights, we've brought you fights. Talk, hype. Linus leans into some pickup's bed. Waiting, watching. The ones who've laid money whoop in places. So do others. And it goes, it waxes and wanes. The voice behind the microphone is a pro. Familiar.

There is a time. Quiet. Nothing. They all know what comes; facts, odds, the rest. But here there is quiet. A buzz begins. Questioning, cursing. Then anger, then fear. The speaker is quiet still. A hum coming. What is this, what is this.

There is a pop. Floodlights at the border. The crowd's form shivers like an anthill kicked. Scared shouting and stumbling. Linus crawls under the line. Screams and pops. Maybe guns, something else. He tries to rise. A large man in a small suit directs arrests from atop the hood of a long square car the color of old blood dried. Blue adorned goons flooding among scared attendees. A small man in a large suit leans to whisper to his comrade above. An exodus floods out. Linus lets himself be lost among the flow of arms and legs windmilling their way through a chaotic funnel away. Spinning lights. The bullhorn cough bark of God knows. Howls now. More pops. Maybe guns, who can know. People duck or kneel. Cars kicking up dirt, fuck this. Linus stumbles. A ping. Maybe a bullet. Dutch is there. Reporter. A laugh. Shirt grabbed. Come on, come on. More laughter. There is a boom somewhere, and laughing, and awe, and then they are in the coupe, and they are peeling away and vanishing among those few who know these backroads enough to become properly lost.

They sit at the counter. Linus, Dutch. The man in the paper hat is there. Counting out the day's take. Some ungodly hour. The scent of burned coffee hangs in the air. Each man has a cup at his front. Styrofoam, small. A penny each. Dutch's foot bouncing. He checks his watch, he checks his phone.

Hydraulic whoosh and sigh. Jeremy Red steps through the door. The overlarge hat comes off, tossed on the countertop.

"You serve food?"

The paper hat man looks up but doesn't speak.

"Donuts," says Dutch.

"My God."

Jeremy Red sits.

"Coffee, garcon. Line em up."

The man brings a Styrofoam cup like the rest. Red drinks and winces and sets the cup down. Linus writes in his notepad. Dutch stares straight ahead.

"They picked up Benny."

Red turns.

"You saw?"

Dutch says he did.

"Who else?"

"Nobody who matters. Spectators."

"Were they coming for us?"

"I don't know. Doesn't look like."

"But they got Benny."

"Maybe just because. He was out in the middle."

Jeremy Red drinks his coffee. Making a face after gulps. He sets the cup down empty.

"You think Harvey gave us up?"

"Would he bother?"

"No reason."

"Yeah."

Red swirls a finger over the empty cup. The paper hat man brings another and takes away the first.

"What time is it?"

Dutch checks his watch and tells him.

"Okay. Go get Benny out. Bring him back to the shop."

"Now?"

"They're open for us. Get him out. Bring him back."

Dutch nods and stands. He straightens his person and leaves a tip and he turns to the door. He speaks without looking back.

"Are you coming?"

Linus closes his notepad and follows.

———

She leads them along. The strawberry clerk. She doesn't look back to see if they follow. Long hallways, old carpet. Then a door and a keypad, and now she does look back, pressing numbers. A buzz and a thump, and she brings out a long iron key and she uses this too, and now the door opens, and now they move on.

The room is sprawling. A series of cages made from cinched chain link. Padlocks on some. Huddled forms looking out. A few in some, more in others. Dutch steps in, stretching, looking over heads. Scanning this way and back. He points, he says that one. The strawberry clerk digs through keys.

"Okay. There are some forms."

She opens the cage and the referee moves through those souls left behind. She locks it back in place and she peels through a series of files hanging from a wall. Dutch steps near and they talk. The referee hovering and shamed.

Linus wanders close. The caged look up dejected. A horror zoo. In among them a man shuffles cards. He looks up at Linus and looks away again. Cards shuffling. Linus stands watching. The man cuts cards. He slides one off the stack and holds it facedown.

"Do you want to see?"

Linus watches the hand laid atop the card.

"Will it matter?"

The dealer shrugs, eyes falling closed.

"Too soon to say."

A moment. Then.

"I'll let it ride."

The dealer nods. He cuts the cards again and lays the top half over the one and moves it to disappear in the deck. Still Linus lingers, watching.

"Reporter."

Dutch shouting.

"You come or you stay."

The main door is open now, and they are going, Dutch, the referee. Linus stops at the door with the clerk.

"Is Harvey still over in admin?"

"Harvey?"

"The newspaper."

"Oh hon. Okay. No. That man's in big boy jail now."

———

They sit in talk. Dutch on seat's edge, the referee looking at the floor. Little gestures from Dutch. A kind of pleading in its way. The other man barely moves. Listening if even that.

The shop is still besides. Dimmed lights at most. All the stacks dark. The radio on the table plays some honky tonk thing. This machine. It looks old-timey but the dials tune into a signal of digital make. Satellite beam. Antenna all pretend. Jeremy Red sits in a chair. He nudges Linus alongside.

"Do you know what he's saying?"

Pointing at Dutch and the referee.

"I can take some guesses."

"We have a kind of problem."

Linus nods. He says hmm. Red is leaning back. Pointing still. We're a small business. This is a moment. A dynamic event. Lots of this talk. Righting the ship. A chance. And Everett. A chance there too. Meant to be. Did they arrest him? If not. Meant to be. More pointing. Red sips a drink. Maybe a nip, who knows. He gestures hard as he talks and he sips. He says are you on board? When the time comes. Linus says yes. He says I'm on board. It goes. The songs change. A moment.

"This song."

Linus looks at the faux vintage radio.

"You like this song?"

"I don't know it."

Jeremy Red drinks. He gestures with his glass.

"That is the answer to a different question."

And.

"Listen to it. Let yourself hear what that man says. Hear what he felt. Close your eyes."

He closes his eyes.

"There you go. You hear it?"

"I hear the song."

"Good. Now open them."

He drinks his drink. The glass thumps down hard.

"You're never gonna hear that song again. The world is always fading, don't convince yourself it's not. These old songs are ghosts. Are you understanding me?"

"About the songs."

"About the songs. About the world."

Dutch is turning. He puts up a thumb for show. Jeremy Red turns to Linus.

"You're sure now."

"Sure of what?"

"You're a scribe. You're here to keep an account of things. No matter what happens."

"I can do that."

"Can you do that?"

"I can."

Dutch is there, he's leaning to speak, but Jeremy Red waves him away. He reaches for his glass but it remains empty on the table and he sets it back again. For a moment everything is still.

"When's the last time you heard Waylon Jennings on the radio?"

9. Raid on Alton Everett

The back door stands open onto the morning alley. The referee is there smoking, pacing. Tapping out a cigarette on the sole of his shoe and lighting another. Filter bent and hot dropped into a pocket.

Jeremy Red leans back. A song playing on the little radio. His eyes are closed as he speaks.

"No one's gonna get hurt. He's an old man."

Linus turns pages and writes. Pen moving fast now.

"We're just scaring him. We don't need guns for that."

An engine comes. A car moving along the alley. The referee drops his cigarette on the ground. Red sits forward.

"You steal a car. You don't take your car."

Linus writes in his notepad. Red watches him.

"You gonna be okay with this?"

"I am a witness."

"You are a witness."

"I am a scribe."

"There you go."

The car out there idles. A rumble unhurried.

"Is he a witness?"

Linus points at the alley where the referee has moved from view. Jeremy Red follows the line.

"Benny? Lord no. He has a higher calling."

And.

"If we end up in jail you can put it in your book."

The radio plays. A song ends and a man comes on. He speaks about better things to come, just wait, just wait. Those days are only just beyond the next turn. Then a touch of news tacked on after the rest. A body found in a river. Some transient, no one. Jeremy Red turns off the radio.

———

Traffic whistles in its constant passing. Cars and cars and cars. The men sit parked and for some moments nothing happens. Then Jeremy Red is pulling from a trash bag instruments which he hands around to each man.

"What is this?"

"Put them on. There's a purpose here greater than you."

They pull on burlap sacks over their faces and they twist and adjust holes to fit eyes. He asks if they're good and they start to respond and then he is out of the car, he is crossing the open lot to the roadside museum.

"Fuck it," one of them says, none could say who, and they pour forth from the car and follow the path on that Jeremy Red has laid. The referee, Linus. Dutch watches from behind the wheel.

When they enter the railcar there stands a spectacle. Two women are paused. Bleach hair poofed, one-piece bathers, jean shorts pulled high. Their faces are tight, empty, ready to let out a scare they still process.

Beyond them Alton Everett glares with eyes hard and narrow and done.

Then the world is moving, all things are happening at once. The referee is urging the women aside, and Red is moving, he is pointing at the display holding the gun, he is shouting, get it open, get it open. Linus stands fixed by the door.

The women first whisper. Then their voices raise. They push, they bicker. One is shit scared, the other is mad. They tussle, they get louder still. The referee watches, captured by their dawning drama, laughing, and he is watching still as the back of his head explodes outward.

The two women embrace. One makes a sound. A whimper. Alton Everett holds the gun from the case. He is turning, he is pointing it at Linus. Jeremy Red curses and he moves and he grabs at the gun, he pulls and Everett pulls and they struggle and there comes in the little room the loud boom of another gunshot. The world again pauses. Red yanks the gun. Everett slips, he falls. Red looks around. Blood spills from his middle.

"You fuck," he says, and he shoots Alton Everett dead with that antique pistol.

10. Stories and Gossip pt. 2

The drive back is quick but it is long. Jeremy Red says it worked, he says it's fine. He says he can't believe it all came together. He laughs. Then he is quiet. Dutch turns the dial. A new song plays. Upbeat guitar, saxophone. A readout runs with words. Bill Haley and the Comets. Red stirs, he tells him to change it.

"We're going to listen to this, Mister Red."

After that Jeremy Red is quiet again.

———

They park in the alley at a slant. The car coasts and stops and will move no more. Linus is sitting. Dutch watches in the mirror. Jeremy Red is still.

"I'm going to check the car."

"What?"

Dutch shifts in his seat.

"I'll be right back."

He steps out, and his door stays standing open, and Linus is here now alone with the quiet and the moment and the dead. When the coupe starts up it is a boom between alley walls. It moans and it idles and then it is growling and moving and gone. Still Linus sits. If he says words in this time no one hears. He looks to Jeremy Red. This man is gone. Linus pats the man's leg. He collects things he must and steps from the car.

The back door is not locked. He enters the shop and moves through a room quieted. No song is here, no light. He passes on into the day beyond and finds the shuffle of traffic moving about in the downtown afternoon. Car horns booping, doors slamming. Life stretching and grasping and sighing and living.

He taps the diner's window. A patron turns and then another. He goes in. A small waiter steps over.

"Is the waitress working?"

"I'm sorry?"

"Is she in?"

"Sir. Sir, we have a lot of waitresses."

The skulls of dead cows look on. Patrons one by one turn away. A man among them unkempt. Hair disheveled and face unshaved in god knows. But he wears the fine oxfords of a man well. The watch on his wrist fits a little loose. Expensive. A coat hangs over an empty chair at his table, long and fine cut from the yellow flesh of some thing. This man nods and he cuts meat and fat forked for a bite from a slab chopped from a creature engineered of much the same and he gives the slightest of nods but he too at last turns away as all the rest do.

Linus looks around. He says to the small waiter I'm sorry, and the waiter only looks on, and Linus says I'm sorry, sorry. He turns from the waiter and the patrons and the decades gone cows and steps back out onto the walk. The bell chimes wrong and then the door is closed. He breathes here, standing.

A car is parked along the lane. Right up against the curb. This thing square and long, the color of old blood. A man steps out and then another. The big one talks.

"I know you."

His suit is too small. Stretched and bizarre on every seam of his person.

"Don't I know you?"

Linus only shrugs. He says I don't think.

"No," says the big man. "No. I know you."

The little man behind. He smiles too much. Too much. He leans and he reaches and speaks words that are for the big man alone. Nodding now. Yes.

"I know you," he says again.

Linus nods. He says maybe. Around here. Around here maybe. The big man stares. The small man grins. His suit hangs off his small frame. There is a moment. Long. Waiting.

A nod comes. Someone among them, but they all do in their way, little nods from each, and then this is done. Linus moves on.

The man in the paper hat looks away. Eyes down as Linus enters the coffeeshop. He moves on by in quick step. Stairs lead up. The little apartment above. The world below goes on with its clink of dishware and its performative scents, but here Linus exists alone and immediate, separate and apart from the thousand thousand goings on, the deluge of moments spilling forever onto some vague idea of now. Here Linus is. Here he exists. From some pocket he produces an antique gun, a Colt 1911, which he lays on the room's little desk, and he brings the old typewriter out to set at its side. He inserts paper and he rolls the wheel through satisfying clicks, and only now does he sit down to collect these men's stories.

Craig Rodgers is the author of several books, a handful of lies, and all manner of foolishness.

Death of Print Titles

Consumption & Other Vices, a novel by Tyler Dempsey
Awful People, a novel by Scott Mitchel May
The Sun Still Shines on a Dog's Ass by Alan Good
Drift, a novel by Craig Rodgers
The Ghost of Mile 43, a novel by Craig Rodgers
One More Number, stories by Craig Rodgers
Francis Top's Grand Design, stories by Craig Rodgers
Francis Top's Lost Cipher, stories by Craig Rodgers